AuthorHouse™
1663 Liberty Drive
Bloomington, IN 47403
www.authorhouse.com
Phone: 1 (800) 839-8640

Because of the dynamic nature of the Internet, any web addresses or links contained in this book may have changed since publication and may no longer be valid. The views expressed in this work are solely those of the author and do not necessarily reflect the views of the publisher, and the publisher hereby disclaims any responsibility for them.

This book is printed on acid-free paper.

ISBN: 978-1-7283-6094-2 (sc)
ISBN: 978-1-7283-6093-5 (e)
ISBN: 978-1-7283-6095-9 (hc)

Library of Congress Control Number: 2020908175

Print information available on the last page.

Published by AuthorHouse 05/06/2020

author HOUSE®

THE
ADVENTURES
of
Kamille

The Adventures of Kamille

Mr. Larry's Lollipop Shop in Amsterdam

By Gina Frierson-Reed

This book is dedicated to my children Kamille and Khloe and my nephew Andre (AJ). I thank God for blessing me with you! It's an honor and blessing to be your mother and auntie. I love you to the moon and back. Thanks to all those who gave me encouragement along the way on my journey of writing for children.

I'm off to an adventure to see what I can see. I'll save the day however with happiness and glee!"

Kamille sang as she climbed up the ladder to her backyard treehouse, with her magic chest tied around her waist.

I'm excited to see what adventure the magic chest will take us on next," said Kamille as she sat in the middle of her treehouse.

She then heard a knock at the door.

"Kamille! Its AJ and Khloe!"

"We couldn't wait to play with the magic chest," said Khloe.

"Hopefully we don't go too far away this time," said AJ.

"Wherever we go, we know how to get back," said Kamille.

"Yes, we do," said Khloe.

"Skip away, skip a roo! Count to three and home we'll be!" shouted Khloe.

"That's right, that's exactly what my nana told us to say," said Kamille.

"1-2-3!" they shouted as they struggled to open the chest.

The chest popped open and a tornado twister of glitter circled around them creating a barrier they could not see beyond.

As the glitter fell away, they were standing in a small village with large brick buildings. In front of them stood a store called Mr. Larry's Lolly's.

"Wow, it's amazing," said Khloe.

"What a candy store!" said Kamille.

"I bet you they have delicious gum drops, lollipops, and licorice in all flavors," said AJ, as he gazed toward the store, mesmerized by its beauty.

"Let's go inside and see what they have," said Kamille.

The candy store was breath taking, with over a hundred glass jars filled with different flavors of lollipops, gum drops, and jelly filled candies.

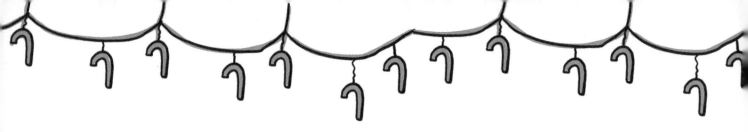

A tall slender man wearing black pants, a red and white stripped hat, and apron stood on a ladder filling jars one at a time from a bag full of jelly-filled candies.

"Hallo! Sorry we zijn niet open," said the man, as he turned around and smiled.

"I don't understand what he just said," whispered Khloe.

"Me neither," whispered AJ.

"Excuse me, sir, can you tell me where we are?" shouted Kamille.

"You don't have to shout," said the man laughingly. "I speak Dutch and English," said the man as he started climbing down the ladder.

"You're at Mr. Larry's Lolly's in Amsterdam."

"Amsterdam!" shouted Khloe.

"Wow," said AJ.

"My name is Mr. Larry. What are your names?" asked Mr. Larry.

"I'm Kamille and these are my friends, Khloe and AJ," said Kamille.

"Well, its very nice to meet you. Welcome to my candy store," said Mr. Larry.

"You have an incredible candy store," said Kamille.

"Yes! It's amazing," said AJ.

"Thank you," said Mr. Larry. "I'm glad you think so, but business hasn't been so good lately."

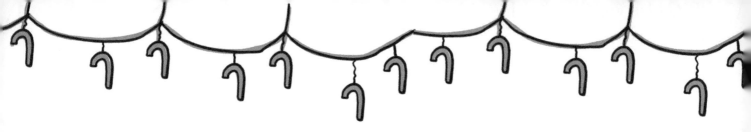

"I make my lollipops from scratch, and the last batch I made the children say they aren't sweet enough."

"They aren't sweet enough?" asked AJ.

"That's what they say, AJ," said Mr., Larry.

"It was painful for me to taste the sweetness of the last batch because I burned my tongue while tasting some of the jelly for my jelly-filled candies."

"Well, how about you let us judge the sweetness," said Kamille.

"Sure," said Mr. Larry. "Which lollipop would you like to try?"

"I'll try the blueberry," said AJ as he pointed towards the glass jar of blueberry lollipops.

"Can I try the cherry?" said Kamille.

"I want the green apple," said Khloe.

"Hmmm, this one doesn't have much sweetness at all," said AJ. "I can barely taste the blueberry.

"My green apple is sweet, but it could use a sour powder on the outside," said Khloe.

"Well, mine is sweet, but shouldn't cherry be sour?" asked Kamille.

Mr. Larry sighed, "That's what it is, I just can't seem to get the flavor of my lollipops right."

"I have a great idea," said Kamille. "What if you add more sugar to your lollipops and coat each one with a sour coating?"

"Well, I guess it wouldn't hurt to try," said Mr. Larry. "Let's step over to my lollipop station."

Mr. Larry lifted the top lid.

"Here is where we add more sugar," said Mr. Larry as he added more sugar then closed the lid.

"What flavor should I make?"

"How about grape?" asked AJ.

Mr. Larry turned the nozzle, hit the grape button and out popped a lollipop. Then he rolled it in a sour coating.

"Now give it a try." Mr. Larry handed it to AJ.

"Oh, wow this is amazing," said AJ.

"Can you make more?" asked Kamille.

"Sure," said Mr. Larry.

"These are absolutely divine," said Kamille.

"Yes, they are," said Khloe.

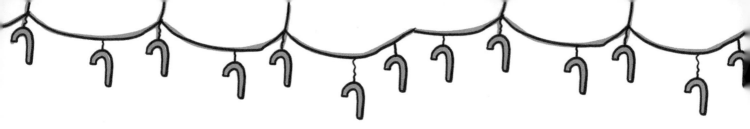

He hesitated a little before tasting the lollipop that looked a little different than the lollipops he normally creates.

As Mr. Larry put the lollipop in his mouth and his face cringed as the sour powder hit his taste buds, and his eyes grew three more sizes.

"Delightful!" said Mr. Larry. "This taste is amazing!" "Now I have to figure out how to spread these throughout the village so they will know Mr. Larry's Lollipops are the best in Amsterdam."

How about we take free lollipops outside for the children to try?" asked Kamille

"Sure, I think it's a great idea," said Mr. Larry. "I will go and make more."

"Khloe ran over to the strawberry licorice.

"This is so fruity and delicious," said Khloe.

Kamille and AJ ran to the gum drops.

"These are tasty!" said Kamille.

After he had piled three buckets full of lollipops, Mr. Larry handed them to the three friends, along with store uniforms.

"Here are lollipop stands, hats, and aprons for you to represent the store," said Mr. Larry.

"Well, how can we say free lollipops in Dutch?" asked Kamille.

"Lolly's!" "Lolly's!" "Krijg je gratis Lolly's," said Mr. Larry.

"This means "Lollipops!" "Lollipops!" "Get your free Lollipops," said Mr. Larry.

"How about you say it in English, and I can say it in Dutch," said Mr. Larry. "Most of the people in this village can understand and speak English very well and they will understand us both."

"Lollipops! Lollipops!" they shouted as they burst out the door. "Get your free lollipops!"

"Lolly's!" "Lollys!" "Krijg je gratis Lolly's!" shouted Mr. Larry as he stood in the doorway of the store.

A crowd began to gather to taste the colorful and flavorful candy.

"Tasty," said a little girl in the crowd.

Kamille glanced over at Mr. Larry. He dotted tears from the corner of his eyes as he watched the crowd grow.

The children began to stream inside the store, and Mr. Larry went behind the counter to greet them.

"Come on, friends, I'm going to need your help," said Mr. Larry.

Kamille, Khloe, and AJ went behind the counter to help Mr. Larry.

"Okay," said Kamille.

"Druif," said a little boy.

"That means grape," said Mr. Larry.

"Kers," said a little girl.

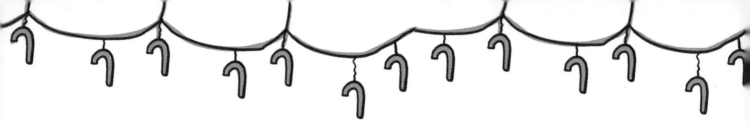

"That means cherry," said Mr. Larry.

Soon the grape lollipops began to run out.

"Oh no!" "I'm getting low on lollipops and I can't make more and run the register at the same time," said Mr. Larry.

"Well, I saw how you made them Mr. Larry, and I'm sure I can make them without a problem," said AJ.

"That would be great," said Mr. Larry. "Let me know if you need any help."

AJ walked through the crowd of children anxiously shouting out what flavor lollipops they wanted.

He lifted the lid added sugar and closed the lid hit the grape button and out popped a lollipop. Then he rolled it in sour coating, AJ continued to make more until he had three buckets full.

"Thank you so much, kids!" said Mr. Larry. "I couldn't have done this without you."

"You are very welcome!" said Kamille.

Soon the crowd began to slow down.

"Well, Mr. Larry, it looks like its time for us to return home," said Kamille.

"Thanks for helping me today," said Mr. Larry. "If you're ever in the area again feel free to stop by and get a free lollipop."

"Thank you!"

"See you later, Mr. Larry," they said while waving goodbye as they walked out of the store.

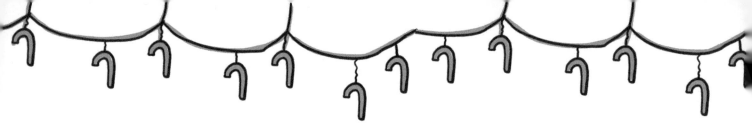

"It looks like we helped Mr. Larry save the day," said Kamille.

"Yes, it was an unforgettable experience," said AJ. "But we must head back home."

"Before Mom comes and checks on us," said Khloe.

"Okay on a count to three," said Kamille.

"Skip away, skip a roo, count to three and home we'll be!" "1-2-3!" they shouted.

With a twister of glitter, they were back at the treehouse.

"That was wonderful," said AJ.

"This magic chest is the best," said Khloe.

"See you later Kamille," said Khloe and AJ as they left the treehouse.

"I'm off to an adventure to see what I can see. I'll save the day however with happiness and glee," Kamille sang as she carried her magic chest home.